PUFFIN BOOKS

The Puffin Book of Heroic Failures

Here at last is the long-awaited, U-certificate *Puffin Book of Heroic Failures*.

On the following pages are failures of all kinds, performed by people, animals and machines. The only thing they have in common is . . . they all went wrong! So sit back and prepare yourself for the greatest discovery in the world: everybody fails at something!

All of the tales in this book have been taken from the (really grown-up) *Book of Heroic Failures* and the (really groan-up) *Return of Heroic Failues* – both of which have been a HUGE success!

The Western world is crazy about success, even though most people find failure much easier to achieve. The author, Stephen Pile, used to be the President of the Not Terribly Good Club of Great Britain. Unfortunately, the club came to an end in 1979 after 20,000 people applied to become members. The Club was felt to be too successful – it had failed to be a failure.

Stephen Pile

The Puffin Book of

Heroic Failures

Illustrated by Alan Rowe

PUFFIN BOOKS

PUFFIN BOOKS

Published by the Penguin Group
Penguin Books Ltd, 27 Wrights Lane, London w8 5tz, England
Viking Penguin, a division of Penguin Books USA Inc.
375 Hudson Street, New York, New York 10014, USA
Penguin Books Australia Ltd, Ringwood, Victoria, Australia
Penguin Books Canada Ltd, 10 Alcorn Avenue, Toronto, Ontario, Canada M4V 3B2
Penguin Books (NZ) Ltd, 182–190 Wairau Road, Auckland 10, New Zealand

Penguin Books Ltd, Registered Offices: Harmondsworth, Middlesex, England

This collection first published 1991
10 9 8 7 6 5 4 3 2 1

Printed in England by Clays Ltd, St Ives plc
Filmset in Monophoto Plantin

Contents

Contents

That's Show Business

Least Successful Pop Records

During the 1970s a new singing phenomenon brought out three records.

One was called 'I'm a Pirate King', which, before demand slumped, sold eleven copies. 'I was knocked out when I heard,' the performer said. 'It's going to be a great hit.'

He improved upon this when his next single, 'The Cuckoo Clock', sold three copies. His most memorable record, however, was a version of 'Old King Cole' with a heavy synthesizer backing. It sold one copy worldwide.

'I'm going to be a star,' the singer observed. To us, of course, he already is.

The Worst Orchestral Tour

In August 1977 the London Sinfonietta visited Tunisia to give two concerts at the Tabarka and Carthage Music Festival.

On landing at Tunis Airport they found that the courier, who was to transfer them by bus to Tabarka, was not there, nor was the bus. Eventually, the courier did turn up, but there was still no sign of the bus and it was two hours before they embarked upon a hair-raising journey to the Mimosas Hotel, where twenty rooms were reserved. On arrival the hotel had, naturally, never heard of them nor of the Carthage and Tabarka Music Festival.

The orchestra spent the night on the beach without bedclothes, pillows, food or drink in huts belonging to a disused Club Méditerranée. Coincidentally, Mr Michael Vyner, the orchestra's artistic director, dreamed of his mother advising him to become a lawyer and to avoid the world of professional music.

Next day, no one in Tabarka knew anything about a concert that night or any other, and the Carthage end of the festival 'seemed not to care one way or the other what was happening in their sister town'. The orchestra abandoned the first concert, played the second and returned to Heathrow Airport with a deep sense of gratitude.

The Worst Orchestra

The worst orchestra ever to perform in public was the Portsmouth Symphonia. Formed in 1970, two-thirds of its members had never touched an instrument before.

This factor above all others made their renderings of the light classics so refreshingly original. Unhampered by preordained melody, the orchestra tackled the great compositions, agreeing only on when they should start and finish. The cacophony which resulted was naturally an immense hit and before long they made two long-playing records. These became very popular, demonstrating yet again the public's great appreciation of incompetence. Leonard Bernstein said that the Portsmouth Symphonia changed his attitude to the William Tell Overture for ever.

The Least Successful TV Programme

In 1978 an opinion poll showed that a French TV programme was watched by no viewers at all.

The great day for French broadcasting was 14 August, when not one person saw the extensive interview with an Armenian woman on her fortieth birthday. It ranged over the way she met her husband, her illnesses and the joy of living.

The poll said that 67 per cent had preferred a Napoleonic costume drama and 33 per cent had opted for 'It's a Knockout'.

The programme was transmitted at peak-viewing time and was selected in the previous day's *France Soir* as the best programme on the channel that evening.

The Most Unsuccessful TV Commercial

The comedienne Pat Coombs is the proud holder of the record for the largest number of unsuccessful 'takes' for a television commercial. In 1973, while making a breakfast cereal advertisement, she forgot her lines twenty-eight times. On each occasion she forgot the same thing – the name of the product. When asked five years later what the product was, she replied: 'I still can't remember. It was some sort of muesli, but the name was practically unpronounceable. They were very kind to me, but that only made it worse. I had total stage fright every time the camera came near me. With each take I got worse. It's put me off cereal for life.'

The commercial was never finished and the product was taken off the market soon afterwards.

The Least Successful Fringe Show

The Edinburgh Festival fringe was set alight in 1983 by an outstanding production of *Ubu Roi* that closed after only fifteen minutes of its first and last performance.

Advance publicity whetted the appetite for 'the first appearance in Britain by an extraordinary West Berlin ensemble (Freie Theateranstalt) with a pig, cockatoos and several parrots who create a visual symphony and a threatening stillness'.

The leading actor and director, Hermann van Harten, said the production did not have the animals as advertised because no one told him they would have to be put into quarantine. The parrots and cockatoos were dispensable, but the pig was essential because it played the role of Ubu Roi's wife. At the last minute they had borrowed a pig called Rust from the local East Lothian city farm and the play's opening was delayed for five days due to intensive pig training.

On the big night Rust just 'oinked around the

place', refusing to jump up and down as the part required.

After only a quarter of an hour on the opening night van Harten passed out on stage with exhaustion. A member of the cast then stepped forward to say that the show was so awful they had decided to scrap it and give everyone their money back.

The Most Pointless Radio Interview

One of Britain's most popular radio programmes is 'Desert Island Discs', in which a celebrity is asked to imagine that, for unspecified reasons, he or she is trapped on a desert island with eight favourite records.

In the early 1970s the programme's presenter, Roy Plomley, was keen to get the novelist Alistair Maclean on to his programme. As a writer of adventure stories, it was felt he might fit the role of a castaway and give a gripping broadcast. This was soon arranged, despite Maclean's known reluctance to give interviews.

Mr Plomley arranged to meet him for lunch at the Savile Club in London. They got on extremely well.

During lunch Mr Plomley asked, 'Which part of the year do you put aside for your writing?'

'Writing?' said Maclean.

'Yes – your books – *Guns of Navarone*.'

'I'm not Alistair Maclean, the writer.'

'No?'

'No. I'm in charge of the Ontario Tourist Bureau.'

With no alternative, the two set off for the studio. During the recording an increasingly agitated producer urged: 'Ask him about his books.' 'He hasn't written any,' replied the broadcaster.

The programme was never broadcast.

The Least Interesting Live TV Show

In April 1986 the WGN TV station got a scoop. Amidst much ballyhoo they announced they were going to unseal Al Capone's secret vault beneath the Lexington Hotel, Chicago. It was said to contain hoards of missing money, diamonds, whisky and the bones of those who had 'upset' him.

Entitled 'The Mystery of Al Capone's Vaults', the two-hour live show was hosted by an excited reporter who wore an excavation helmet and a large fighter-pilot's moustache. 'I am Geraldo Rivera and you're about to witness a live television event,' he gasped. 'Now for the first time that vault is going to be opened live. This is an adventure you and I will take together.'

The show was syndicated across the whole of America and there was a carnival-like atmosphere, with hundreds celebrating at an 'Al Capone Safe-Cracking Charity Ball'. Also in attendance was a small army of law enforcement officials, reporters,

Internal Revenue agents, members of the federal treasury, claiming that Capone still owed them $800,000, and criminal technicians, who were there gathering evidence.

To add an air of authenticity to the production, Rivera demonstrated the use of a prohibition-era Thompson sub-machine gun and detonated a dynamite blast using a Capone-style plunger.

Tension mounted as an explosives team arrived. After an hour and a half blasting through walls, the dust settled and the cameras went in, accompanied by Dr Robert Stein, the County Medical Examiner, who was on hand in case bones or mummified bodies were found.

The vault contained two empty gin bottles and Geraldo filled in the time by singing 'Chicago'.

The Least Successful Conducting

Although he composed a few symphonies, Hector Berlioz is mainly notable for conducting a concert from which the orchestra left before the end.

It was a rule at the Theatre Italien that musicians did not have to stay beyond midnight. Five to twelve approached and, due to the evening's exquisite chaos, only three-quarters of the ambitiously long programme had been completed.

The clock chimed twelve. Berlioz turned to conduct the last work, his own *Symphonie Fantastique*, and found that only five violins, two violas, four cellos and a trombone remained.

The delighted audience clamoured for them to play the symphony anyway, but Berlioz explained that this was not possible with five violins, two violas, four cellos and a trombone. 'It is not my fault,' he said in one of the great quotations of musical history. 'The orchestra has disappeared.'

The Least Solemn Mass

Beethoven's *Missa Solemnis* was given its most dramatic performance ever at Acton Town Hall in March 1988. Professor James Gaddarn, of Trinity College of Music in London, was gathering Ealing Choral Society and Orchestra to launch into the profoundly beautiful notes of the final movement when there was a sudden crash. A door slammed at the back of the hall and you could have heard a pin drop.

In the hush Professor Gaddarn, who had his back to the audience, felt a prickle of anxiety. 'I heard this commotion. It was like a horse coming down the aisle. I heard footsteps behind me coming towards the rostrum.'

He turned round and there was this apparition: a spaceman in glittering silver helmet, black leggings, chains, heavy gauntlets and big boots.

'What on earth do you want?' hissed the professor. Mumble, mumble, said the spaceman, but the professor was unable to understand a word. 'It eventually tumbled out that he was from a kissogram agency.

By quick cross-examination I was able to discover that he had come to the wrong hall.'

Clank, clank. Away clumped the spaceman. The professor raised his baton and completed the enjoyable work.

The Least Accurate Newspaper Report

Newspaper reporters make mistakes, of course, but few have been more innovative than the one who contributed a personality profile of a local man called 'Harris' to the *Wiltshire Times and Chippenham News* in 1963. The following week the paper carried a magnificent apology.

Mr Harris, it said, has asked us to point out a number of inaccuracies in our story. After returning from India, he served in Ireland for four years and not six months as stated; he never farmed at Heddington, particularly not at Coate Road Farm as stated; he has never counted cycling or walking among his hobbies; he is not a member of fifty-four hunts; and he did not have an eye removed at Chippenham Hospital after an air raid on Calne.

'My only disappointment when interviewing him,' wrote the reporter in his original article, 'was that I could not spare more time with this raconteur.'

The Smallest-Ever Audience

The smallest audience on record is two. They attended Mr W. H. C. Nation's pantomine *Red Riding-hood* at Terry's Theatre in London at the turn of the century. The audience were both up in the gallery and they declined an offer to come down and sit in the stalls. As a result the cast did not see a single person throughout the show. What happened when they divided the audience in half to sing along with the villain and the hero can only be imagined.

The Worst Song Entry

Singing an entrancingly drab number called 'Mile after Mile', a Norwegian pop singer, Mr Jan Teigan, scored nil in the 1978 Eurovision Song Contest. The voting from the panels all over Europe was unanimous: 'Norway – no points; nul points; keine Punkte.'

Next morning the papers were naturally full of Mr Teigan, pushing mention of the actual winner, Izhar Cohen, into a subsidiary paragraph. After the contest press photographers had crowded round our hero, giving him star treatment. 'This was my greatest success,' he said. 'I have done what no one ever did before me. I'm the first Norwegian to get zero points. After the concert I had to make sixty splits for the photographers and I've got lots of offers for TV appearances, tours and interviews. I've never known as much interest taken in me.'

The Least Successful Song Writer

For twenty years Mr Geoffrey O'Neill has been writing what he calls 'good catchy tunes that people remember and whistle'. In this time he has composed 501 songs and three musicals. Not one of them has been recorded, published or performed by professionals.

Mr O'Neill, who comes from Great Dunmow in Essex, files all his songs away in case there should be a sudden demand for them. He cheerfully reports that song number 102 is called 'Try, Try Again', while number 332 is entitled 'People Think I'm Stupid'. An oil firm employee, he gives public lectures on how unsuccessful his songs are.

The Most Misprints in a Newspaper

This record is claimed for a page in *The Times* of London on 15 March 1978; it contains seventy-eight misprints.

One story starts, 'Sir Harold Wilson's action in making public a oss' and goes on to deal with a braodcast involving the governm and comparahle pay claims.'

These errors were caused by an industrial dispute and do not, in any case, have the sheer style of the *Guardian*, which can do this sort of thing quite unaided. Among its most famous misprints was a review of the opera *Doris Gudenov*.

The Least Successful Newspaper Competition

In May 1986 the distinguished British journalist Henry Porter revealed that he had planted five deliberate grammatical errors in his *Sunday Times* column and would send a bottle of champagne to any reader who spotted them all correctly.

Letters poured in by the sackload. The next week Mr Porter announced that readers had found not one of the five mistakes. However, they had located a further twenty-three of which he was not aware.

This overtakes the previous best. In 1964 the *Carmel Independent* in California printed a school photograph and asked readers to identify which child became a well-known celebrity. While cropping the picture for publication, an enthusiastic sub-editor cut out the child in question, making it impossible to win the contest from merely looking at the paper.

The Least Satisfactory Performance of *The Sound of Music*

Only the South Koreans have really got to grips with *The Sound of Music*, the well-known film in which Julie Andrews and a selection of carbolically scrubbed infants burst into song up Alps, inside monasteries, on assorted staircases and in a wide range of wholly surprising locations.

Finding the film a shade overlong, the Koreans wisely decided to cut out all the songs. Shown with no music whatsoever, yet still called *The Sound of Music*, the film proved extremely popular and played to full houses all over South-East Asia.

The Least Successful Agony Aunt

This honour falls to the outstanding Rose Shepherd, who wrote the agony column in *Honey* magazine in 1980. From the day of her appointment onwards she did not receive a single reader's letter. When, months later, a few actually did arrive, this fine woman announced that she could not solve any of them.

'They asked impossible questions like, "I eat cigarette tobacco. Is this wrong?" It was hopeless.' Deciding that people's problems are basically insoluble, she resigned.

The Least Successful Audience Participation

The growing trend towards audience involvement has given us all the opportunity to add to theatrical confusion.

During 1974 a young woman attended a performance of the rock musical *Godspell* in London.

During the interval, the cast invited members of the audience up on the stage to meet them. She is said to have left her seat, walked down the arcade outside and passed through the stage door. After climbing a flight of dark stairs, she turned right and found herself on a brilliantly lit stage.

To the great surprise of herself and everyone else, she found herself in the middle of the cast acting *Pygmalion* at the theatre next door.

The Least Successful Weather Forecast

At the end of a bravura weather forecast in October 1987 Mr Michael Fish told British TV viewers that 'a woman rang to say she'd heard there was a hurricane on the way. Well, don't worry. There isn't.' Brushing aside this fanciful amateur forecast with a chuckle, the immortal Fish predicted 'sea breezes' and a 'showery airflow'.

In no time Britain was hit by 120 mph winds that ripped up 300 miles of power cables, plunged a quarter of the country into darkness, blocked 200 roads with fallen branches, felled 25 per cent of the trees in Kent and stopped all rail traffic in the south of England for twenty-four hours. An ambulance at Hayling Island was hit by a yacht floating across the road and the Meteorological Office said it was the worst hurricane since 1703.

A spokesman for Mr Fish later said: 'It is really all a question of detail.'

The Least Successful Weather Report

After severe flooding in Jeddah in January 1979, the Arab News gave the following bulletin:

'We regret we are unable to give you the weather. We rely on weather reports from the airport, which is closed because of the weather. Whether we are able to give you the weather tomorrow depends on the weather.'

The Least Successful Fun Festival

In October 1980 Chichester hosted a fun festival that promised 'a weekend that was different'. The organizers kept their word.

The British all-comers dog swimming race was called off when not a single owner entered their pet; the pie-eating contest was won by a man who consumed just three and a half pies; the helicopter rides were cancelled because of bad weather; the parachute display was called off because the landing-site was too close to the A27; and the Elvis Presley lookalike, 'Rupert', was delayed by a road accident, and when he eventually arrived there were so few spectators the act was shelved.

When by three o'clock nothing had happened at all, a lively crowd formed around the organizers' tent. Inexplicably, they were not enjoying this feast of entertainment. Loud among the voices of complaint was Mr R. Farncombe, who had come all the way from West Worthing:

'I went mostly to see Rupert who was not there, for a helicopter ride we never got and wrestling which did not exist. Thank goodness we didn't arrive till twelve thirty.' He was offered free tickets for the next day when the high spot was a hot-air balloon which failed to turn up.

The Most Boring Lecture

The previous record holder was Dr David Coward. In 1977 he won the 'Most Boring Lecturer of the Year' contest at Leeds University with an exquisitely dull talk on 'The Problems of the Manned Urinal'. In March 1986, however, he was outclassed by Dr Frank Oliver of Exeter University, who delivered an unbeatable lecture on 'Coefficiency Correlations'.

With his back to the audience throughout, he explained in a series of comprehensively detailed blackboard diagrams exactly how to 'measure the strength of the relationship between two variables at points between minus one and plus one'. It is a subject which, Dr Oliver says, is 'essentially fascinating'.

So resounding was his triumph in this annual competition that the event was cancelled the following year. No one on the staff felt confident to pit themselves against the reigning title-holder.

When the event was revived in 1988 Dr Oliver won yet again by the simple device of repeating exactly the same lecture.

The Least Successful Sound Effect

In 1944 King Haakon of Norway delivered a rousing wartime address to his beleaguered people on the BBC World Service. As His Royal Highness was running forty seconds short, the producer sent to the library for a fanfare to round things off. At this point the talk came brilliantly alive.

Haakon had just commended his country to God, made a few Nordic farewell grunts and laid down his script when the air was suddenly alive with the sound of roundabouts and ribaldry and cockneys shouting, 'Roll up, roll up, ladies and gentlemen.' The library had sent a funfair. Afterwards, the king said it was 'the sort of thing that happens'.

The Least Successful Circus Act

When the circus came to New York in 1978, the publicity posters carried the question: 'Can aerialist Tito Gaona – spinning at 75 miles an hour – accomplish the most difficult acrobatic feat of the twentieth century?' The short answer to this was, 'No.'

Every night for nine months Tito attempted the first-ever quadruple somersault in mid-air from a flying trapeze 60 feet above the ground. Every night for nine months he got part way through, missed his catcher and plunged into the safety net. At Madison Square Gardens he sustained a whole season of magnificent failure. Asked if he had ever done it, Tito replied: 'Yes, once. At rehearsals and only my family were watching.'

The Least Successful Contortion Act

As part of his act while appearing in Roberts Brothers Circus at Southend in August 1978, Janos the Incredible Rubber Man was lowered to the floor hanging from a trapeze, with his legs wrapped somewhere behind his head. Normally, he rolls around for a spell to the applause of amazed audiences, before reverting to a more conventional human posture.

On this occasion he just sat there. 'I couldn't move,' he said later, by way of explanation.

The situation was resolved by a circus official, Mr Kenneth Julian. 'We put Janos in the back of my van and took him to hospital.' Doctors wrestled with the problem for thirty minutes and ordered the Incredible Rubber Man to lie flat for a week.

The Least Successful Human Cannonball

In 1972 Miss Mary Connor made three fearless attempts to become the first woman ever to be blasted across the River Avon.

On the first occasion the cannon fired and nothing happened. On the second the cannon went off at half-cock and she swept gracefully into the air, getting at least half-way across the river.

However, her personal best came on the third attempt, when she arrived, wearing a bandage round her ankle and plasters on both elbows, while explaining to bystanders that she had grazed them coming out of the cannon. She not only flew out this time and went into the river, back first, at exactly the same spot, but also capsized the rescue boat and had to swim to the bank.

This entirely surpasses the previous record, held by Miss Rita Thunderbird, who remained in the cannon while her bra was shot across the River Thames.

The Least Successful Exhibition

The Royal Society for the Prevention of Accidents held an exhibition at Harrogate in 1968. The entire display fell down.

The Most Overdue Library Book

The most overdue book in the history of library services was a copy of Dr J. Currie's *Febrile Diseases*. It was taken out of the University of Cincinnati Medical Library in 1823 by Mr M. Dodd and returned on 7 December 1968 by his great-grandson.

In the intervening period it had accrued a fine estimated at 2,646 dollars (then £1,102).

The Slowest-Selling Postcard

The world's slowest-selling postcard depicts a fascinating fourteenth-century Tibetan rain-bucket.

The inspired publications officer at the Victoria and Albert Museum had 5,000 copies of this exquisite card printed. Of these twenty-four were destroyed in a flood and 4,972 are still available. Only four were ever sold . . .

A Special Award for the Post Office

After a long and expensive advertising campaign the Great British people were still glowingly unacquainted with their postcodes. In desperation the Post Office decided to launch a quiz in September 1985. There was only one question and to get a prize you merely had to get your own postcode right.

Happily, few of the replies got through. When giving their address the Post Office got their own postal code wrong. 'It was a printing error,' said the head postmaster, modestly declining to bask in the glory.

The Least Successful Baton Twirling

Noted for the height, range and drama of their twirls, members of the Ventura Baton Twirling Troupe surprised even themselves on one occasion in the late 1960s.

During an Independence Day march past, one of their batons hit a power cable, blacked out the area, started a grass fire and put the local radio station off the air. 'They were on form,' the mayor said.

The Worst Magician

It is quite possible that if Tommy Cooper's tricks had worked, no one would have heard of him. Happily, however, his magic was, from the start, blessed with an almost operatic badness. He became a much-loved household name.

It may be of interest to hear how this great man discovered his unique gifts. At the age of seventeen, while an apprentice shipwright, he appeared in a public concert held in the firm's canteen at Hyde in Essex. Intending to give a serious display of magic, he walked on to the stage. As soon as the curtains parted, he forgot all his lines.

For a while he just stood there, opening his mouth only to close it again. The audience was spellbound. All right, he thought, get on with it.

He got on with it and everything went wrong. His grand finale was the milk bottle trick. 'You have a bottle full of milk,' he told the entranced audience, 'and you put paper over the top. You turn the bottle upside down, and take the paper away. The milk stays in.'

With bated breath, the audience watched. He turned the bottle. He paused for effect. He took away the paper. Drenched. All over him.

As if he had not done enough already, Mr Cooper then got stage fright and began working his mouth furiously without any sound coming out. At this point he started to tremble and walked off, perspiring heavily. Once in the wings, he heard the massed cheers of a standing ovation. His future glory was assured.

Snippets

'We don't like their sound. Groups of guitars are on the way out' – Decca Recording Company when turning down the Beatles in 1962 (the group was also turned down by Pye, Columbia and HMV).

'Far too noisy, my dear Mozart. Far too many notes' – Emperor Ferdinand after the first performance of *The Marriage of Figaro*.

If At First You Don't Succeed . . .

The Most Unsuccessful Attempt to Work Through a Lunch Hour

Mr Stanley Hird surely set a record in June 1978 when trying to catch up on some paperwork. At one o'clock his carpet factory outside Bradford was deserted and he settled down for an uninterrupted hour. At ten past one a cow fell through the roof. The cow had clambered on to the roof from the adjoining field. For thirty seconds they stared at each other and then the cow, who had also been planning a quiet lunch hour, lowered her head and charged. This continued for some minutes, during which time Mr Hird retreated steadily towards the door as the cow scattered stacks of wool. Eventually the heifer, whose name was Rosie, stopped to chew a green carpet and Mr Hird escaped into the corridor. Here he met a farmer who inquired if he had seen a heifer. Police, firemen and an elaborate set of pulleys were needed to extract the animal.

The Least Successful Nurse

While serving on the wards of King's College Hospital, London, in 1987, a student nurse saw a frail, elderly woman seated upon the edge of a bed. 'Time for your bath,' said the good nurse. 'I've already had one,' replied the old woman, who showed signs of confusion.

With kindly firmness she led the old woman to her bath, took off her clothes and washed her thoroughly. On returning to the ward, the nurse said, 'Someone else has got into your bed.'

'It's my sister,' replied the old lady. 'I've come to visit her.'

The Least Successful Kamikaze Pilot

During the last world war a Japanese Kamikaze pilot made no less than eleven suicide flights. Although he set off with enough petrol for a one-way trip, no weapons of self-defence and the ritual farewell from his commanding officer, he came back safely each time and went on to write an autobiography in which he claimed that the planes were unsafe.

A member of the Japanese Special Attack Corps, he lived till he was ninety-three.

The Worst Spy

Reversing the usual outcome of spying, Mr R. E. de Bruyeker gave the other side copious details about himself.

He broke into the NATO naval base at Agnano, near Naples, while spying on behalf of the Soviet Union in 1976 and removed a box of top-secret documents.

He played his masterstroke when he left his overnight bag behind in the office. It contained not only a hammer, a file, a Bible and a copy of *Playboy*, but also full details about himself and his whereabouts. He was traced almost immediately.

The Least Successful Hunter

In 1985 a hunter went duck-shooting in New Zealand. A less fair-minded man would have fired both barrels at the duck, causing unnecessary carnage. With a keen sense of justice, however, our man fired both barrels and missed, whereupon the duck circled round, dive-bombed, knocked him over and shattered his glasses.

The Least Successful Oil Drillers

Erecting the very latest equipment, Texaco work-men set about drilling for oil at Lake Peigneur in Louisiana during November 1980.

After only a few hours' drilling they sat back, expecting oil to shoot up. Instead, however, they watched a whirlpool form, sucking down not only the entire 1,300-acre lake, but also five houses, nine barges, eight tug boats, two oil rigs, a mobile home, most of a botanical garden and 10 per cent of nearby Jefferson Island, leaving a half-mile-wide crater. No one told them there was an abandoned salt mine underneath.

A local fisherman said he thought the world was coming to an end.

The Least Successful Santa Claus

In 1983 happy children had just left Santa's grotto amidst much yo-ho-hoing when police walked in, clapped Father Christmas in handcuffs and frog-marched him out through the toy department at Allders store in Croydon. Amazed goblins who assist in the grotto said that Santa was 'taken to the police station and charged with persistent non-payment of traffic fines'.

The Least Successful Divers

In 1979 a West Country subaqua club gained permission to dive in Britain's most inaccessible loch. Happy in the knowledge that they were the first-ever people to explore the underwater world of remotest Scotland, they drove 740 miles, climbed 3,000 feet, put on their gear and plunged in to find that it was only 4 feet deep.

The Least Successful
Archaeological Discovery

In one of the most exciting archaeological finds of the century a team of researchers in Tehran uncovered the skeleton of a dinosaur which had hitherto been found only in North America.

The ribs and vertebrae were carefully preserved and in 1930 a scientific mission from Madrid flew out to conduct a thorough examination.

Things got even more exciting when their final report announced that the reptile was, in fact, an abandoned hay-making machine which had been caught in a landslide.

The Least Successful Attempt to Solve the Mystery of the Loch Ness Monster

All attempts to find the Loch Ness Monster have failed. No one has failed more magnificently than the four Hemel Hempstead firemen who in 1975 tried to seduce it.

Believing that feminine wiles would lure the beast from the deep, they built a 30-foot-long *papier mâché* female monster, equipped with long eyelashes, an outboard motor and a pre-recorded mating call. 'Sex solves everything,' said one of the firemen.

Painted blue and green, the monster then set off in search of romance with two firemen inside steering. They travelled fifteen miles offering flirtation and mystery, but encountered only sustained hormonal indifference from the deep. There are two possible reasons.

First, the firemen learned that their pre-recorded mating call was that of a bull walrus and so unlikely to interest the Ness beast.

Second, the outboard motor developed a fault during the voyage. The monster went into a flat spin, veered off backwards and crashed prostrate across a jetty.

No girl is at her best under these circumstances.

The Least Successful Demolition: 1

Margate pier was declared dangerous in 1978 after violent gales had lashed the Kent coast. It was thought best to pull the pier down before it collapsed.

In January 1979 the demolition team arrived and detonated an immense charge of gelignite. The explosion sent water hundreds of feet into the air, but left the pier's essential character unchanged. After a second 'demolition' a rivet was found embedded in the wall of a seafront pub and police insisted that all future attempts should be made at high tide. The result was that explosion number four took place at midnight and woke up all Margate's seafront.

The demolition team made six further attempts before a Margate councillor suggested that, in view of the large crowds they attracted, the unsuccessful explosions should be made into a weekly tourist attraction.

After the fourteenth attempt, the demolition team was retired and a replacement company employed. After attempt number fifteen, the lifeboat house on the pier was seen to be at a slight angle.

The Least Successful Demolition: 2

In December 1980 Solihull Council hired a local firm of contractors to demolish a row of delapidated cowsheds on the Stratford Road near Birmingham.

Early on Sunday morning eyewitnesses saw an

excavator moving at speed along the road. When it came to the cowsheds, it turned off on the wrong side and headed without pause for Monkspath Hall, a listed eighteenth-century building set in fields with a tree-lined approach and rated as one of the most famous farmhouses in the Midlands.

In forty-five minutes the building was reduced to a heap of rubble.

The Worst Canal Clearance

In 1978 workers were sent to dredge a murky stretch of the Chesterfield–Stockwith canal. Their task was to remove all the rubbish and leave the canal clear. They were soon disturbed during their teabreak by a policeman who said he was investigating a giant whirlpool in the canal. When they got back, however, the whirlpool had gone and so had a one-and-a-half-mile stretch of the canal. In its place was a seamless stretch of mud, thickly punctuated with old prams, bedsteads and rusting bicycle accessories. In addition to this the workmen found a flotilla of irate holiday-makers stranded on their boats in a brown sludge.

Among the first pieces of junk they hauled out had been the 200-year-old plug that alone ensured the canal's continuing existence. 'We didn't know there was a plug,' said one workman, explaining that all the records had been lost in a fire during the war. 'Anything can happen on a canal,' a spokesman for the British Waterways Board said afterwards.

. . . Don't Try Again!

The Man Who Almost Invented the Vacuum Cleaner

The man officially credited with inventing the vacuum cleaner is Hubert Cecil Booth. However, he got the idea from a man who almost invented it.

In 1901 Booth visited a London music hall. On the bill was an American inventor with his wonder machine for removing dust from carpets. The machine comprised a box about 1 foot square with a bag on top. After watching the act – which made everyone in the front six rows sneeze – Booth went round to the inventor's dressing room.

'It should suck not blow,' said Booth, coming straight to the point.

'Suck?' exclaimed the enraged inventor. 'Your machine just moves the dust around the room,' Booth informed him. 'Suck? Suck? Sucking is not possible,' was the inventor's reply and he stormed out. Booth proved that it was by the simple expedient of kneeling down, pursing his lips and sucking the back of an armchair. 'I almost choked,' he said afterwards.

The Least Successful Defrosting Device

The all-time record here is held by Mr Peter Rowlands of Lancaster, whose lips became frozen to his lock in 1979 while blowing warm air on it.

'I got down on my knees to breathe into the lock. Somehow my lips got stuck fast.'

While he was in the posture, an old lady passed and inquired if he was all right. 'Alra? Igmmlptk,' he replied, at which point she ran away.

'I tried to tell her what had happened, but it came out sort of . . . muffled,' explained Mr Rowlands, a pottery designer.

He was trapped for twenty minutes ('I felt a bit foolish') until constant hot breathing brought freedom. He was subsequently nicknamed 'Hot Lips'.

The Least Satisfactory Robot

Seeking greater efficiency, the Kavio Restaurant in Leith bought Donic, a robot programmed as a wine waiter. In the summer of 1980 they dressed it in a black hat and bow tie, fitted the batteries and turned on.

Showing a natural flair for the work, this advanced machine ran amok, smashed the furniture, poured wine all over the carpet and frightened the diners until its light went out, its voice-box packed up and its head dropped off in a customer's lap. When asked to account for this outstanding performance, the robot's manufacturer said that he had given the operating instructions to the restaurant's disc jockey.

The Worst Computer

It is widely suggested that computers improve efficiency. Lovers of vintage chaos might remember the computer installed in 1975 by Avon County Council to pay staff wages.

The computer's spree started off in a small way, paying a school caretaker £75 an hour instead of 75 pence. Then it got ambitious and did not pay a canteen worker at all for seven weeks.

Before long it got positively confident and paid a janitor £2,600 for a week's work. He sent the cheque back and received another for the same amount by return of post.

There was now no stopping it. A deputy headmistress received her year's annual salary once a month, heads of department earned less than their assistants, and some people had more tax deducted in a week than they earned all year.

In February 1975 280 employees on the Council payroll attended a protest meeting. Of these, only eight had been paid the correct salary. They all went on strike.

The Worst Deaf Aid

During a visit to his doctor in March 1978, Mr Harold Senby of Leeds found that his hearing improved when the aid which he had been wearing for the past twenty years was removed. 'With it in I couldn't hear much,' he said. 'But with it out I had almost perfect hearing.'

Closer medical examination revealed that in the 1950s a deaf aid mould was made for his left ear instead of his right. 'Over the years I have been fitted with several new aids, but no one noticed that I had been wearing them in the wrong hole.'

The Greatest Mathematical Error

The Mariner I space probe was launched from Cape Canaveral on 28 July 1962 towards Venus. After thirteen minutes' flight a booster engine would give acceleration up to 25,820 m.p.h.; after forty-four minutes 9,800 solar cells would unfold; after eighty days a computer would calculate the final course corrections and after 100 days the craft would circle the unknown planet, scanning the mysterious cloud in which it is bathed.

However, with an efficiency that is truly heartening, Mariner I plunged into the Atlantic Ocean only four minutes after take off.

Inquiries later revealed that a minus sign had been omitted from the instructions fed into the computer. 'It was human error,' a launch spokesman said.

This minus sign cost £4,280,000.

The Least Successful Firework

The most unsuccessful firework so far ignited was the 'Fat Man' Roman candle, perfected in 1975 by Mr George Plimpton of New York. It weighed 720 pounds, was 40 inches long and was developed to break the record for the most spectacular firework ever. It succeeded admirably.

Lighting it, Mr Plimpton confidently predicted that it would reach an altitude in excess of 3,000 feet. Instead of this, however, it hissed, whistled and blew a 10-foot crater in the earth.

The Most Unsuccessful Firework Display

The reign of King James II got off to a fine start when a stately firework display was organized on the River Thames the day after his coronation. As the first one was lit, an over-enthusiastic spark gave premature encouragement to the rest. One of the most spectacular firework collections of the century was gone inside a minute. There was a simultaneous banging and whizzing so great that dozens of spectators jumped into the Thames and for hours afterwards the city of London was full of coachmen chasing their runaway horses.

The Least Successful Experiment (Involving a Bat)

Charles Waterton, the great Victorian traveller, devoted many years to the study of vampire bats. For reasons of scientific thoroughness, he felt that his research would not be complete until he had been attacked by one. To this end he arranged to sleep with just such a bat in his bedroom, while allowing his big toe to peep forth from the hammock.

After many weeks engaged in this venture Waterton remained woefully unbitten, unlike his Indian servant, Richard, who was nightly ravaged until he became too weak to perform his duties. 'His toe,' Waterton later complained bitterly, 'held all the attractions.'

The Least Successful Experiment (Not Involving a Bat)

A pioneering French inventor called Sauvant claimed in 1932 that he had perfected the world's first crash-proof aeroplane. From all accidents, he said, the aircraft and passengers would emerge completely unscathed.

On three occasions gendarmes removed the wheels from this contraption to prevent Monsieur Sauvant taking off in something that looked like a metallic boiled egg with prongs.

The irate inventor said it was perfectly safe and based upon his own experiments showing that if a hen's egg is placed inside an ostrich egg, the chicken embryo would be unaffected by the experience. As one French paper said: 'No explanation of how the smaller egg is placed inside the larger one has yet appeared, nor have we been told what fate befalls the ostrich.'

Eventually, Monsieur Sauvant persuaded several friends to push him off an 80-foot cliff in Nice. Confident that they would see him step out triumphantly waving, they peered down at the beach to see a total wreck shattered beyond all hope of reconstruction and an inventor too dazed to leave his vehicle without the assistance of ropes and a team of enthusiastic admirers.

Later, when he had recovered, he declared that he was delighted with the success of the experiment.

The Most Unsuccessful Inventor

Between 1962 and 1977 Mr Arthur Paul Pedrick patented 162 inventions, none of which was taken up commercially.

Among his greatest inventions were 'A bicycle with amphibious capacity', spectacles which improved vision in poor visibility and an arrangement whereby a car may be driven from the back seat.

The grandest scheme of Mr Pedrick, who described himself as the 'One-Man-Think-Tank Basic Physics Research Laboratories of 77 Hillfield Road, Selsey, Sussex', was to irrigate deserts of the world by sending a constant supply of snowballs from the Polar regions through a network of giant pea-shooters.

He patented several golf inventions – including a golf ball which could be steered in flight – that contravened the rules of the game.

Going Places?

The Least Successful Learner Driver

Now that Mrs Miriam Hargreaves, the world record holder, has let us all down by passing her driving test at the fortieth attempt, the field becomes wide open for a promising newcomer. Many doubters felt, however, that her dazzling total of 212 lessons would be unsurpassed. O ye of little faith . . .

By March 1980 the sprightly Mrs Betty Tudor of Exeter had been learning for nineteen years and had clocked up a breathtaking 273 lessons. In this time she had nine instructors and was banned from three driving schools. She put in for only seven tests and failed them all with flying colours.

Her seventh ended when she drove the wrong way round a roundabout, whereupon the examiner screamed at her and said that he would drive from then on. Mrs Tudor told him that if it hadn't been for the cars coming in the opposite direction, hooting, he wouldn't have noticed anything wrong.

Although Mrs Tudor has now decided to sell the car, one suspects that she is only resting. You cannot keep a talent of that magnitude down for long.

The Fastest Failure of a Driving Test

Until recently the world record was held by Mrs Helen Ireland of Auburn, California, who failed her driving test in the first second, cleverly mistaking the accelerator for the clutch and shooting straight through the wall of the Driving Test Centre.

This seemed unbeatable until 1981 when a Lanarkshire motor mechanic called Thomson failed the test before the examiner had even got into the car. Arriving at the test centre he tooted the horn to summon the examiner, who strode out to the vehicle, said it was illegal to sound your horn while stationary, announced that Thomson had failed and strode back in again. Genius of this kind cannot be taught. It is a natural gift.

The Least Successful Safe-Motoring Competition

Wishing to enhance their country's reputation for careful driving, the French held a safe-motoring contest in 1987. The plan was to award free petrol tokens to motorists who impressed roadside police with their respect for the law and concern for others.

After several days they had still not awarded a single prize and so the police decided to lower their standards. Hereafter they would give the tokens to any driver who was obeying the basic traffic regulations. Even this proved difficult.

When gendarmes tried to flag down the first winner, he assumed he was in trouble and raced away. When they signalled for the second winner to pull off the road, he accelerated through a red traffic light and the police had to book him instead.

In the end they gave the award to anyone they could find with a current driving licence whose car was fitted with a seat belt.

The Least Satisfactory Garage

The least satisfactory garage in the history of covered car parking adjoins a semi-detached house at Elkwood, Templelogue, in Dublin.

In 1978 prospective buyers of Mr Donal O'Carroll's home were intrigued to see that four concrete steps led up to the garage.

The estate agent handling the sale said, 'I understand the driveway was very steep, which was why the steps were put in. The garage is ideal for anyone wanting an extra room, but certainly not if you want to park your car.'

The Least Successful Garage

The previous record holder merely had a garage with four steps up the front. However, in a fearless advance in garage design Mrs Caroline Hitchens decided to incorporate one in the basement of her 'dream home', built on a hillside in Penzance.

Any car parked in this garage would have needed to cross the lawn and several flower beds and then descend a 30-foot cliff to the road. To get out at the back of the house the car would have to burrow up through 30 feet of earth to join the traffic.

The Worst Attempts at Car Repairs

In 1976 a travelling salesman had bought a new car and for fully twenty-four hours its performance was perfect in every respect. However, by the following day, all its forward gears had jammed.

'I was too busy at the time to get it fixed,' he said. As the reverse gear was still in good order, our man decided that thereafter he would drive everywhere backwards. 'I have covered 80,000 miles since then.'

The Least Successful Car

Ford produced the car of the decade in 1957 – the Edsel. Half of the models sold proved spectacularly defective. If lucky, you could have got a car with any or all of the following features: doors that wouldn't close, bonnets and boots that wouldn't open, batteries that went flat, hooters that stuck, hubcaps that dropped off, paint that peeled, transmissions that seized up, brakes that failed and push buttons that couldn't be pushed even with three of you trying.

In a stroke of marketing genius, the Edsel, one of the biggest and most lavish cars ever built, coincided with a phase when people increasingly wanted economy cars. As *Time* magazine said: 'It was a classic case of the wrong car for the wrong market at the wrong time.'

Unpopular to begin with, the car's popularity declined. One business writer at the time likened the Edsel's sales graph to an extremely dangerous ski-slope. He added that, so far as he knew, there was only one case of an Edsel ever being stolen.

The Least Successful Fire Station

Roused by the alarm, the firemen of Arklow in County Wicklow raced to their posts in December 1984, only to find flames completely engulfing their own fire station. 'Christmas is always a busy time for us,' Mr Michael O'Neill, the Chief Fire Officer, said, explaining why the fire had raged unnoticed.

'The lads found their equipment and protective clothing had been destroyed and we watched the station burn to the ground,' he said philosophically. It was the second time Arklow fire station had burned down in recent years.

The Least Successful Fire Engine

In 1973 a fire broke out at 2 Crisp Road, Henley. The occupants telephoned the local fire brigade, only to find that it was taking part in 'Operation Greenfly', a simulated exercise to douse an imaginary fire on the village green.

The alarmed occupants next telephoned nearby Wallington Fire Station, who said they would send a fire engine immediately. Half-way down Bix Hill, the cab burst into flames and the firemen struggled out, choking.

Although there were 400 gallons of water on board, this could not be used, since the suction pump was operated from the cab, which was now full of smoke.

At this point the local fire brigade, on its way back from Operation Greenfly, drove past. They pulled to a halt and said they had very little water left, having just waterlogged the village green.

They did what they could, while the Wallington firemen sheepishly asked passing motorists if they had any fire extinguishers.

The fire at 2 Crisp Road was put out by energetic locals throwing water.

The Worst Aircraft

Among such craft one holds a special place: Count Caproni's Ca 90. Like an immense houseboat with nine multi-layered wings and eight engines, it was launched on Lake Maggiore in January 1921. An Italian historian said it 'would not have looked out of place sailing up the English Channel with the Spanish Armada'.

The test pilot was a Signor Semprini and his nervous doubts were overruled by Count Caproni, who ordered him to take off with a ballast load equivalent to sixty passengers.

Semprini revved his 3,200 h.p. engines and rose up off the lake. Monstrously unstable, the nose dipped briefly, with the result that the ballast rolled to the front of the plane, the wings snapped and the Ca 90 plunged into the water.

The Worst Ship

Between 1953, when it was built, and 1976, when it sank, the *Argo Merchant* suffered every known form of maritime disaster.

In 1967 the ship took eight months to sail from Japan to America. It collided with a Japanese ship, caught fire three times and had to stop for repairs five times.

In 1968 there was a mutiny and in 1969 she went aground off Borneo for thirty-four hours. In the next five years she was laid up in Curaçao, grounded off Sicily and towed to New York.

In 1976 her boilers broke down six times and she once had to travel with two red lights displayed, indicating that the crew could no longer control the ship's movements because the steering and engine had failed. She was banned from Philadelphia, Boston and the Panama Canal.

To round off a perfect year she ran aground and sank off Cape Cod, depositing the country's largest oil slick on the doorstep of Massachussetts.

At the time of the final grounding the ship had been 'lost' for fifteen hours. The crew was eighteen miles off course and navigating by the stars, because modern equipment had broken down. What is more, the West Indian helmsman could not read the Greek handwriting showing the course to be steered.

A naval expert afterwards described the ship as 'a disaster looking for somewhere to happen'.

The Worst Bus Service

Can any bus service rival the fine Hanley to Bagnall route in Staffordshire? In 1976 it was reported that the buses no longer stopped for passengers.

This came to light when one of them, Mr Bill Hancock, complained that buses on the outward journey regularly sailed past queues of up to thirty people.

Councillor Arthur Cholerton then made transport history by stating that if these buses stopped to pick up passengers they would disrupt the timetable.

The Least Successful Balloon Flight

In 1823 Mr Charles Green, the pioneer balloonist, climbed into his basket and lit the take-off fire. The balloon rose slowly, but due to an oversight or a practical joke the ropes were inadequately tied. The result was that the basket stayed behind on the ground. Rather than remain in it, Mr Green and a colleague clung on to the balloon hoop. Thus dangling, they floated over Cheltenham.

The Worst Transatlantic Yachtsman

Crossing the Atlantic single-handed is a challenge attempted by only the greatest yachtsmen and women. The most important of these for us is the immortal Mr Sebury, who made two historic attempts.

On 31 August 1986 he set sail from Newport, Gwent, in a 15-foot sloop specially equipped with a bucket full of cheese, five litres of orange juice and an Ordnance Survey map of the Welsh coast. Three days later he found himself adrift with his mast down and engine broken. He got just beyond the Bristol Channel, where he became a martyr to seasickness and moored the boat in the middle of a Royal Naval Torpedo range. When an official craft went out to warn him, they found Mr Sebury slumped on the side of his vessel shouting: 'Take me ashore and sink the boat.'

Encouraged by this, he made a second attempt to cross the Atlantic later that year and got as far as Milford Haven.

The Worst Hijackers

We shall never know the identity of the man who in 1976 made the most unsuccessful hijack attempt ever. On a flight across America, he rose from his seat, drew a gun and took the stewardess hostage.

'Take me to Detroit,' he said.

'We're already going to Detroit,' she replied.

'Oh . . . good,' he said, and sat down again.

Few other cases come anywhere near this. In 1967 a drunk Arab hijacked a plane and demanded that he be taken to Jerusalem. For his own safety, the crew explained there was a war on there and, being an Arab, he would probably get shot on sight. 'He was so drunk he had to be protected,' the captain said afterwards.

The Least Successful Warship

In times of war self-sacrifice is a paramount virtue. New heights were achieved in 1941 by HMS *Trinidad* when it fired a torpedo at a passing German destroyer. While sailing in the Arctic, its crew completely overlooked the effect of the icy water on oil in the torpedo's steering mechanism. The crew watched as it travelled at forty knots towards its target and slowly became aware that the torpedo was starting to follow a curved course. In less than a minute it was pursuing a semi-circular route straight into the *Trinidad*'s path. Displaying the precision timing on which naval warfare depends, the torpedo scored a direct hit on the ship's engine room and put HMS *Trinidad* out of action for the rest of the war.

The Least Successful Naval Repairs

In September 1978 a paint scraper worth 30 pence was accidently dropped into a torpedo launcher of the US nuclear submarine *Swordfish* and jammed the loading piston in its cylinder. For a week divers tried to free the piston while *Swordfish* was waterborne, but all attempts failed. She had to be drydocked and subsequent repairs cost 171,000 dollars (£84,000).

The Least Successful Target Practice

As part of a training exercise off Portsmouth in 1947, the destroyer HMS *Saintes* was required to fire at a target pulled across its bows by the tug *Buccaneer*.

It fired a shell, missed the target and sank the tug.

The Least Successful Attempt to Shoot Down Enemy Planes

The high spot of the Royal Air Force activities during the Second World War occurred at RAF Castle Bromwich in 1943. When airmen heard a plane landing late at night, they assumed it was one of many Spitfires tested there. Switching on an Aldis lamp, however, Aircraftman R. Morgan observed that it was a German bomber. As it taxied down the runway, he expressed the intention of having a crack at it with the Lewis gun and went off to get permission.

While the German plane revved its engines, Aircraftman Morgan tried to ring through to control. 'We had to crank like fury on the field telephone for permission to fire,' he said. By the time he got through the plane had taken off and was *en route* for Germany.

The Most Unsuccessful Nine-Gun Salute

Rounding Cape Horn, the yacht *Adventure*, entered by the Royal Navy for the 1974 Round the World race, was given a nine-gun salute of welcome by HMS *Endurance*, a 3,600-ton ice-breaker.

Part of the sixth shot hit the 55-foot yacht *Adventure* and wrecked its headsails. The ten-man crew, which had just won the previous leg of the race, had to spend the rest of the day sewing them up.

nd Getting Lost

The Least Successful Day Trip

Few people have packed more into a day trip than Michael and Lilian Long from Kent, who went to Boulogne in May 1987. On Easter Sunday this adventurous couple went for a short walk around the town. In no time they were spectacularly lost and showing all the qualities of born explorers.

'We walked and walked,' Mrs Long recalled, 'and the further we walked to try to get back, the further we walked away from Boulogne.'

They walked throughout the night and finally hitched a lift next morning to a small village they did not recognize. Here they caught a train to Paris. In the pleasure-loving French capital they spent all their remaining money on catching what they thought was the train to Boulogne. After an enjoyable trip they arrived in Luxembourg at midnight on Monday.

Two hours later police put them on the train back to Paris, but it divided and their half ended up in Basle, an attractive medieval town in the north of Switzerland.

Having no money, they tried to find work, but without success. The rail authorities offered them a free warrant back to Belfort, thinking this was where they had come from, whereupon this intrepid pair walked forty-two miles to Vesoul, hitched a lift to Paris and nearly boarded the train to Bonn in Germany.

Diverted to the right platform, they reached Boulogne a week after they had set out on their walk. When he arrved at Dover, Mr Long said this was their first trip abroad and they would not be leaving England again.

The Most Lost Motorist

Far too many Sunday drivers are happy to pootle around for a weekend hour or two following dull itineraries. Only Mr Joseph Stophel of Dunedin in Georgia has transformed this activity into the adventure of a lifetime.

Announcing that he was going out for a short drive in September 1987, Mr Stophel took a wrong turning and got happily lost in the dense network of twisting backroads. Three days later he was the subject of a nationwide search, with regular bulletins on every radio station.

Seven days later Ms Kathleen Stubblefield passed his car as far away as Indiana. She chased after him and flagged him down. Relaxing at the Stubblefield residence in Blairsville, Mr Stophel said he had travelled 1,700 miles in the past week. It appears that he had motored extensively in several states, including Tennessee, Indiana and Kentucky.

The Least Accurate Map

Few maps offer the adventurous walker quite such varied terrain as the one for the Dales National Park. Described as 'definitive' when it came out in 1969, the map contains a network of footpaths more challenging than anything previously published.

In no time keen ramblers found that one footpath went straight up a cliff face, another passed through the middle of a hospital ward and a third involved crossing the River Ribble in two places without the benefit of a bridge.

In an enthusiastic report the *Guardian* newspaper said that 'any walker determined to follow the line would have had to wade across the river up to his neck, walk for 200 metres along the eastern bank, and then wade back again'.

The Least Accurate Tourist Guide

Holiday makers drove round and round in circles, exploring the West of England fully, thanks to a new map given away free by Godfrey Davis Renta-car and Best Western Hotels in 1983.

It marked Taunton as a surfing centre, even though it is fifteen miles from the sea. Furthermore, it placed a racecourse in the heart of the small Devonshire village of Chudleigh and marked Axminster down as having a grand prix circuit. Underwater activities were symbolized by a racing car and windmills by a pick and shovel.

A Godfrey Davis executive said: 'At least we got the roads right.'

Great Moments in the History of Exploration

Three celebrated explorers were invited to dinner at the Geographical Club in London.

Sir Vivian Fuchs had explored Greenland and East Africa and led the Commonwealth Trans-Antarctic expediton of 1955–8.

Dr John Hemming was director of the Royal Geographical Society and a member of the 1961 Brazilian expedition.

Robin Hanbury-Tenison had crossed South America in a small boat and explored the Indonesian islands, Ecuador, Brazil, Venezuela and the mountains of southern Sahara as well as travelling up Africa and down the Amazon in a hovercraft.

They met at the Royal Geographical Society, just a quarter of a mile from their final destination. Within a mere fifteen minutes they were spectacularly lost in the back streets of Kensington.

The Least Successful Explorer

Thomas Nuttall (1786–1859) was a pioneer botanist whose main field of study was the flora of remote parts of north-west America. As an explorer, however, his work was characterized by the fact that he was almost permanently lost. During his expedition of 1812 his colleagues frequently had to light beacons in the evening to help him find his way back to camp.

One night he completely failed to return and a search party was sent out. As it approached him in the darkness Nuttall assumed they were Indians and tried to escape. The annoyed rescuers pursued him for three days through bush and river until he accidentally wandered back into the camp. On another occasion Nuttall was lost again and lay down exhausted. He looked so pathetic that a passing Indian, instead of scalping him, picked him up, carried him three miles to the river and paddled him home in a canoe.

The Least Mysterious Mystery Tour

In 1971 Mr and Mrs William Farmer of Margate travelled to Wales for their summer holidays. At the start of the week they joined a British Rail mystery tour. It took them straight back to Margate. 'We were expecting the Welsh mountains,' they said afterwards.

'We nearly fell through the platform,' said Mr Farmer on reaching Margate, who had been looking forward to getting away all the summer. Declining a tour of the town, Mr and Mrs Farmer popped home for a cup of tea.

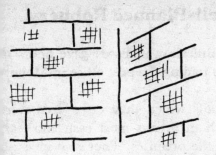

Cops and Robbers

The Least Well-Planned Robbery

Three thieves at Billericay in Essex gave hours of thought in 1971 to raiding the post office in Mountnessing Road.

Among the details which they discovered were the times at which there was most cash and least security guard on the premises. They also invested in masks, guns and a getaway car.

At a pre-arranged time, the Mountnessing gang sped through Billericay and screeched to a halt outside the post office.

It was only when they jumped out of the car and ran towards the building that they discovered the one detail which they had omitted to check. The post office had been closed for twelve years. 'We became a general store in 1959,' said the store's manageress, seventy-six-year-old Mrs Gertrude Haylock. She later remarked: 'I saw these two men running towards the shop with shotguns and I said to my customer, "Here is somebody having a lark."'

Once inside the tiny shop, the raiders pointed their guns at Mrs Haylock and her customer, Mrs Constance Clarke, and demanded the contents of the till.

'I told them we had not taken any money that morning and there was only £6 in the till, so they took that. I should think it was a bit of a disappointment to them. They looked so funny dressed up like that. It was just like in a film.'

After the robbers left, the customer fainted, on realizing that she had been present at an incident.

The Least Successful Bank Robber

Not wishing to attract attention to himself, a bank robber in 1969 at Portland, Oregon, wrote all his instructions on a piece of paper rather than shout.

'This is a hold-up and I've got a gun,' he wrote and then held the paper up for the cashier to read.

The bemused bank official waited while he wrote out, 'Put all the money in a paper bag.'

This message was pushed through the grille. The cashier read it then wrote on the bottom, 'I don't have a paper bag' and passed it back.

The robber fled.

The Least Successful Complaint

In 1975 a thief stole a radio from a shop in Ashton-under-Lyme. When he got home and turned it on, he found that it was defective.

He then went back and demanded that it was repaired free of charge. His request was turned down as he was unable to produce a receipt, so he went round to the police station and complained.

During his interview with the duty sergeant he was charged with theft.

The Most Pointless Bank Raid

With split-second timing and consummate team-work four masked men raided a bank at Artema near Rome in February 1980. Not knowing that the bank had closed three minutes early 'because things were quiet', the gang's leader ran headlong into a locked plate-glass door and knocked himself out.

Falling back into the arms of three accomplices, he was carried to the waiting getaway car and driven off. According to bank officials, this complex raid was completed in just under four minutes.

The Easiest Crimes to Detect

The greatest crimes are marked by a logic and a dazzling simplicity that enables them to be detected almost as soon as they have been committed.

In 1978, for example, Allan Bonds and Bernard Redfearn of Stoke-on-Trent stole a water tank, but forgot that it was still half-full. They left a trail of puddles and got home minutes before the police.

An American robber, Homer Lawyer, held up a bank in Miami. He pushed a note across the counter demanding cash and then fled with a sackful. It was the bank manager who noticed that he had helpfully written his name and address on the back of the note.

Kenneth Peverley made the most of the latest technology while burgling an office in Cardiff, when he knocked over a dictating machine, which switched itself on. He was arrested when police recognized him muttering on the tape.

All of the above, however, are entirely eclipsed by Mr Clive Bunyan, who raided the village store at Cayton, Yorkshire, in 1970, wearing a crash helmet with the words 'CLIVE BUNYAN' written in large gold letters across the front – a definitive performance.

The Noisiest Burglar

A Parisian burglar set new standards for the entire criminal world, when, on 4 November 1933, he attempted to rob the home of an antique dealer. At the time he was dressed in a fifteenth-century suit of armour, which dramatically limited his chances both of success and escape. He had not been in the house many minutes before its owner was awakened by the sound of clanking metal.

The owner got up and went out on to the landing, where he saw the suit of armour climbing the stairs. He straightaway knocked the burglar off balance, dropped a small sideboard across his breastplate and went off to call the police. Under cross-examination a voice inside the armour confessed to being a thief trying to pull off a daring robbery. 'I thought I would frighten him,' he said.

Unfortunately for our man, the pressure of the sideboard had so dented his breastplate that it was impossible to remove the armour for twenty-four hours, during which period he had to be fed through the visor.

The Worst Burglar

The history of crime offers few figures less suited to undetected burglary than Mr Philip McCutcheon.

He was arrested for the twentieth time when, after his latest robbery, he drove his getaway car into two parked vans. During this man's appearance at York Crown Court in 1971, the judge gave a rare display of careers advice from the bench.

Giving our man a conditional discharge, Mr Rodney Percy, the Recorder, said: 'I think you should give burglary up. You have a withered hand, an artificial leg and only one eye. You have been caught in Otley, Leeds, Harrogate, Norwich, Beverley, Hull and York. How can you hope to succeed?

'You are a rotten burglar. You are always being caught.'

The Burglar Who Called the Police

A New York burglar committed what many admirers regard as the perfect crime in 1969. Following a carefully prepared plan, he climbed up on to the roof of a supermarket which he intended to burgle.

Once there, he discovered that he could not enter the building since the skylight was marginally too small to slip through.

With a sudden flash of inspiration he removed all his clothes and dropped them in through the skylight intending to follow them seconds later. Brilliantly, he was still unable to fit through and had to call the police to get his clothes back.

The Least Successful Police Dogs

America has a very strong candidate in La Dur, a fearsome-looking schnauzer hound who was retired from the Orlando police force in Florida in 1978. He consistently refused to do anything which might ruffle or offend the criminal classes.

His handling officer, Rick Grim, had to admit: 'He just won't go up and bite them. I got sick and tired of doing that dog's work for him.'

The British contenders in this category, however, took things a stage further. Laddie and Boy were trained as detector dogs for drug raids. Their employment was terminated following a raid in the Midlands in 1967.

While the investigating officer questioned two suspects, they patted and stroked the dogs, who eventually fell asleep in front of the fire. When the officer moved to arrest the suspects, one dog growled at him while the other leapt up and bit his thigh.

Stealing the Wrong Thing

With a daring that many of their older colleagues could hardly equal, two teenagers broke into a Yeovil grocery shop in April 1984.

Messrs Knibbs and Hunt located what they thought was the cash box, wrenched it from the wall and escaped into the street. When the box started up a shrill buzzing they threw it to the ground and stamped on it, but to no avail. Despite all their efforts to stop the noise this enterprising duo finally had to dump the box in the river. They had stolen the burglar alarm.

The Least Successful Safe-Breakers

Using the latest sophisticated equipment, a gang from Chichester set about cutting open a safe at the Southern Leisure Centre. Happily, it was the wrong sophisticated equipment and in no time they had welded up the door. The manager said that after their good work the safe was so secure that it took three hours to open using hammer and chisel.

The Gang Who Got Lost

At 5 a.m. on September 1981 the Edmonton Two raided the Petro-Canada fuel station in Vancouver, locked the attendant in the washroom and made their getaway with 100 dollars. Coming from Edmonton, they did not know their way around Vancouver and twenty minutes later they drove up at the same petrol station to ask directions.

The attendant, Mr Karnail Dhillon, had just escaped from the washroom and so was alarmed to see the burly pair approaching the cashier's window again. 'They wanted me to tell them the way to Port Moody,' he said. 'I guess they didn't recognize me or the station.'

He was just calling the police when the pair came back yet again to say they could not get their car started. Learning that a mechanic would not be on duty until 8 a.m., they went back to the car and ran the battery down trying to start it. They were on the phone to a towing company when they were arrested by Police Constable Tom Drechsel.

Prompt Police Action

West Midlands police moved swiftly on 15 May 1983, when a caller rang to say there was an abandoned safe on a grass verge at Halesowen. In no time a uniformed officer was on the scene, where he stood guard for over an hour until the arrival of detectives, who dusted it for fingerprints.

This done, they tried taking the safe back to the police station. When all attempts at lifting it failed, the uniformed branch sent a team of constables to help, but even they could not budge it, so the traffic division sent a Land-Rover with towing gear. Man and machine united for twenty minutes of fruitless constabulary-shoving.

'That,' said an officer, 'was when we realized it was a Midlands Electricity Board junction box concreted into the ground.'

The Least Successful Undercover Operation

Two undercover agents from the Spanish Civil Guard spent an evening in 1975 trailing three extremely suspicious-looking characters around Vittoria. At midnight they followed them into a Basque nightclub.

They crossed the dance floor and were just going to pounce when the dubious trio sprang up, put them into half-nelsons and frogmarched them out of the building.

The three were undercover agents from the Civil Guard who had been following the other two all night on the grounds that they looked extremely suspicious.

The Worst Prison Guards

The largest number of convicts ever to escape simultaneously from a maximum security prison is 124. This record is held by Alcoentre Prison, near Lisbon in Portugal.

During the weeks leading up to the escape in July 1978 the prison warders had noticed that attendances had fallen at film shows, which included *The Great Escape*, and also that 220 knives and a huge quantity of electric cable had disappeared. A guard explained: 'Yes, we were planning to look for them, but we never got around to it.' The warders had not, however, noticed the gaping holes in the wall, because they were 'covered with posters'. Nor did they detect any of the spades, chisels, water hoses and electric drills amassed by the inmates in large quantities. The night before the breakout one guard had noticed that of the thirty-six prisoners in his block only thirteen were present. He said this was 'normal' because inmates sometimes missed roll call or hid, but usually came back the next morning.

'We only found out about the escape at six-thirty the next morning when one of the prisoners told us,' a warder said later. The searchlights were described as 'our worst enemy' because they had been directed at the warders' faces, dazzled them and made it impossible to see anything around the prison walls. When they eventually checked, the prison guards found that exactly half the gaol's population was missing. By way of explanation the Justice Minister, Dr Santo Pais, claimed that the escape was 'normal' and part of the 'legitimate desire of the prisoner to regain his liberty'.

The Most Unsuccessful Prison Escape

After weeks of extremely careful planning, seventy-five convicts completely failed to escape from Saltillo Prison in northern Mexico. In November 1975 they had started digging a secret tunnel designed to bring them up at the other side of the prison wall.

On 18 April 1976, guided by pure genius, their tunnel came up in the nearby courtroom, in which many of them had been sentenced. The surprised judges returned all seventy-five to jail.

Great Sporting
Moments

The Worst Goalkeeper

In these days of defensive play it is the general cry that not enough goals are scored. No one has done more to change this situation than Chris Smith, the outstanding goalkeeper of Worthing Boys' Club in 1983.

In only eighteen matches this entertaining player let through 647 goals, an average of 35.9 per game. There were, of course, some days when he did much better than this (he once let in nearer fifty, five of them in seven minutes). 'I don't always see the ball,' he said. 'It goes through my legs.'

Alarmingly, he was sent on a special training course, but his natural gifts could not be tampered with.

If there had been a net on the goalposts and he had not been forced to walk miles picking up the ball each time there is no telling what this fine boy might have achieved.

The Worst Soccer Team

Thanks to the tremendous enthusiasm of boys, this is one of our most hotly contested categories. In 1972 the Norwich Nomads seemed to have it sewn up after a splendid season during which they lost all twenty of their games in the Norwich Boys' League, scoring eleven goals and letting in 431 (an average of 21.55 goals let in per game).

Their mantle was taken over in the 1983 season by the Worthing Boys' Club under-twelve team, which lost all eighteen of their games, scoring only six goals for with an impressive 647 goals against (an average of 35.9 goals let in per game). Widely hailed as the worst team in the country, they were given the annual Worthing award by the mayor for generating national interest in the town. Five years later they still had not won a game.

The Smallest Soccer Crowd

The football match which has attracted fewest supporters was that great game between Leicester City and Stockport County on 7 May 1921. It pulled a crowd of thirteen. This glorious indifference was accentuated by the fact that both teams were playing away from home. Stockport's ground had been temporarily closed and the match was held at Manchester United's immense stadium.

The Worst Soccer Match

In 1973 Oxbarn Social Club football team arranged a friendly match in Germany. It was an opportunity for the lads, who play in the Wolverhampton Sunday League, to get a holiday abroad and also to meet some new opposition. Only when they entered their opponents' luxury stadium did they realize that they had mistakenly arranged a friendly with a top German First Division side. For their part, SVW Mainz were expecting to play Wolverhampton Wanderers, then one of the strongest teams in Britain.

The Oxbarn Club secretary said, 'I thought it looked posh, and when I heard the other side were on an £80 bonus to win, I said to myself, "Something is wrong."'

After the fifteenth goal whistled into Oxbarn's net, their goalkeeper was seen to fall on to his knees. He seemed to be praying for the final whistle. It was around this time that the sixteenth and seventeenth were scored.

Naturally, the Mainz crowd were delighted to watch a team like Oxbarn instead of the mighty Wolverhampton Wanderers. 'They behaved very well,' said the Oxbarn secretary. 'Whenever we got the ball they gave a prolonged cheer.'

Oxbarn Social Club lost 21–0.

The Least Enthusiastic Soccer Team

Blackburn Rovers showed definitive sporting reluctance in their game against Burnley in 1891. In almost perfect conditions (it had been snowing steadily for three hours before kick-off and few fans bothered to turn up) Blackburn let in goals every quarter of an hour and were 3–0 down at half-time.

When the interval went on an unusually long

time, it became clear that Blackburn Rovers did not want to come out at all. Eventually, their team straggled on to the pitch, but the crowd could not help noticing that there were only seven of them.

Ten minutes later, Lofthouse of Blackburn smacked the face of the Burnley captain, who retaliated with a punch. Both players were sent off. Feeling that this was an extremely good idea, the entire Blackburn team decided to follow them, with the exception of the goalkeeper, a Mr Arthur, who remained at his post.

The referee, Mr Clegg, waited a few moments in the hope that Blackburn Rovers might reappear. When they failed to do so, the game restarted with the entire Burnley team bearing down upon Arthur. Nichol scored, but the goalkeeper successfully claimed it was offside and the referee abandoned the match.

The Blackburn captain later explained that this was not a protest against Lofthouse being sent off. They simply wanted to join him and were quite happy for Burnley to have the two points.

The Fastest Own Goal

In an electric start to their match on 3 January 1977, Torquay United set an example that no other league side has equalled. Cambridge United kicked off and Ian Seddon struck a high ball down the length of the pitch, whereupon the brilliant Torquay centre-half, Pat Kruse, leapt above his own defence with lightning reactions. He headed the ball into his own net after only six seconds, scoring the fastest own goal in the history of league football.

A lesser team would have settled for that, but Torquay were on top form. In the forty-fourth minute they increased Cambridge's lead when their full back, Phil Sandercock, powered a spectacular header past his own goalkeeper, Tony Lee, who had been untroubled by Cambridge attacks.

In the second half Torquay slumped and drew level.

The Least Exciting Rugby Match

Colwyn Bay rugby team travelled fifty miles across the mountains of Snowdonia in 1966 to play Portmadoc. However, it was worth the trouble because the game fully surpassed expectations.

The referee ran out on to the pitch with all thirty players, who limbered up, jumped around, sprinted in small circles, touched their toes and generally flexed themselves for action. Only when the teams lined up for kick-off did anyone realize that they did not have a ball.

At this point the game was abandoned.

The Least Successful Rugby Forward

The most tries scored by a rugby player is 250. Our man, however, is Oliver Jones, who scored only three tries in forty-five years of regular play for the Old Edwardian Exiles.

The silver-haired prop forward scored his third try on 15 October 1966, when he was sixty. 'There was a bit of a scramble on the line,' he said. 'I just dropped on the ball. Nothing spectacular.'

Afterwards there was much back-slapping, but Jones didn't let himself go with manly songs and drunken toasts. 'I had to go to my sister's party,' he said.

He used to play rugby because he 'couldn't think of anything else to do on a Saturday'.

The Perfect Match

Keen to play their annual needle match with Nairobi Harlequins in 1974, the fifteen members of Mombasa Rugby Football Club flew 475 miles to Uganda. During the one-and-a-half-hour journey they passed the no less enthusiastic Harlequins team 30,000 feet below, travelling in a fleet of cars to Mombasa. 950 miles later both teams rang to find out what had happened to the opposition.

The Heaviest Defeat in American Football

Sylvia High School shot into the record books in November 1927, when they played a crucial part in their 270–0 defeat by Haven High. In theory it is impossible to score one touchdown every minute but Sylvia don't know the meaning of the word.

Sensing the horribly skilful nature of the opposition, they left the pitch and were half-way to the dressing room when their coach, Frank Brownlee, persuaded them back out. At this point they wisely decided to refrain from tackling anyone or running with the ball should it land anywhere near them.

According to Milliard Kincaid, a Haven player: 'They could have kept the final score down just by taking the ball but they didn't want to do that.'

Of course not. Instead, they all sat down in the middle of the field and got to know each other.

The Worst-Ever Baseball Team

Formed in 1962, the New York Mets were given a ticker-tape welcome down Broadway before they had even touched a ball.

On 13 April the Department of Sanitation band struck up 'Hey, Look Me Over' and 40,000 spectators lined the route as the uniformed players rode past like conquering heroes in a rainbow-coloured procession of fourteen convertibles. Along the route

10,000 mock baseballs and bats were thrown into the crowd.

After this triumphant start they really got cracking and by 22 April they had equalled the Brooklyn Dodgers' 1918 record of losing nine games in a row. And by the end of this great debut they had lost more matches in one season than anyone else in the history of the game. The final figure was an impressive 120 defeats.

The Worst Boxer

Ralph Walton was knocked out in ten and a half seconds in a bout at Lewiston, Maine, USA, on 29 September 1946. It happened when Al Couture struck him as he was still adjusting his gum shield in his corner. The ten and a half seconds includes ten while he was counted out.

The Worst Boxing Debut

In February 1977 Mr Harvey Gartley became the first boxer to knock himself out, after forty-seven seconds of the first round of his first fight before either boxer had landed a punch.

It happened in the regional bantamweight heats of the 15th Annual Saginaw Golden Gloves contest in Michigan, when Gartley was matched against Dennis Outlette. Neither boxer had fought in public before. Both were nervous.

Gartley started promisingly and came out of his corner bobbing, weaving and dancing. As the crowd roared them on, Gartley closed in, threw a punch, missed and fell down exhausted. The referee counted him out.

Marathons Can Be Fun

In 1966 Shizo Kanakuri set a new record for the Olympic marathon. At Stockholm he completed the 26.2-mile course in an unbeatable fifty-four years, eight months, six days, eight hours, thirty-two minutes and 20.3 seconds, having started in 1912.

He had run several miles before passing a group of people having a very pleasant drink in their front garden. As he was suffering from chronic heat exhaustion at the time, he did the only sensible thing and tottered over to join them. Being a sociable sort of man, he stayed for a few more drinks, whereupon he changed his race tactics dramatically, caught a train back to Stockholm, booked into a hotel for the night, boarded the next boat to Japan, got married, had six children and ten grandchildren, before returning to the villa where he had stopped and completing the marathon for the honour of Japan.

Slowest Olympic Athlete

At the 1976 Olympics in Montreal, Olmeus Charles from Haiti was last by the largest margin ever recorded. He set an all-time record for the 10,000 metres race. Giving the crowd tremendous value for money, he completed the course in forty-two minutes, 0.11 seconds. Everyone lapped him at least three times and the winner finished so far ahead that he would have had time to complete another 5,000 metres.

An argument broke out among the track officials as to whether he should be allowed to finish the course. Happily, the crowd was not denied this fine sight and the entire Olympic timetable was held up by fourteen minutes.

The Least Successful Attempt to Break a World Record

At the glorious 1932 Olympic Games the Finnish athlete Iso-Hollo was hot favourite to break the world record for the 3,000 metres steeplechase. Roaring into the lead from the first lap, he was on target for a new time and turned the corner expecting to hear the bell for the final lap.

At this point one of the Olympic all-time greats intervened. The official lap-counter was, in fact, looking the wrong way, being absorbed in the decathlon pole vault nearby. He failed to ring the bell for the last lap and the entire field kept on running.

When he finally got back on the job, Iso-Hollo completed the race in ten minutes 33.4 seconds. It was the slowest-ever time for the 3,000 metres steeplechase, but then, they did run an extra 450 metres.

The Slowest Start to an Olympic Heat

A relaxing start is, of course, essential to anyone who really wants to enjoy a race. The finest such start was achieved by the American athletes Eddie Hart and Ray Robinson, who held the 100-metres world record and would not normally interest us. In 1972, however, they pulled out something a little bit extra, missed the bus from the Olympic village and watched their own race on television. This gave them a much fuller overall sense of the whole event.

The Least Successful Olympic Swimmer

Carolyn Schuler of the USA won the 100-metres butterfly at the 1960 Rome Olympics in a new world-record time. She was, however, completely overshadowed by her team-mate, Miss Carolyn Wood, who dived into the pool, swam one length, turned, disappeared beneath the water and gave every appearance of having become the first swimmer to drown during the Olympic Games.

Miss Wood eventually rose spluttering to the surface and grasped the lane rope, whereupon her coach dived in fully clothed to administer resuscitation. Afterwards she told the eager reporters: 'I got a big mouthful of water and could not go on.'

The Worst Pentathlon Team

Only Tunisia has really explored the possibilities of modern pentathlon, in which athletes show quite unnecessary prowess in five different sports.

At the 1960 Rome Olympics they scored no points at all in the riding event, because the entire team fell off their horses. It was the first time that anyone had scored nought at the Olympics.

Encouraged by this start, they hit sizzling form in the swimming, where one of their people nearly drowned and the versatile Ennachi (who had already fallen off a horse) took twice as long to complete a mere 300 metres as the winner. Their shooting was described as 'wild' and they were ordered from the range because they were endangering the lives of the judges.

When it came to the fencing, only one of their team could do it, so they kept sending the same man out. During the third bout his opponent said, 'I've fought you before,' ripped off his visor and had him disqualified.

Tunisia came a splendid seventeenth out of seventeen. They were a spectacular 9,000 points behind the leaders and scored half as many as Germany, who came sixteenth. It is the lowest-ever pentathlon score and an example to us all.

The Worst Ski Jumper

Few people know who won the 90-metres ski jump at the 1988 Winter Olympics in Calgary. Everyone, however, knows that Eddie 'the Eagle' Edwards came a definitive last, flapping both arms for mid-air balance and complaining that he could not see anything because his pebble spectacles steamed up during take-off.

A plasterer from Cheltenham, he amazed everyone

by deciding to enter the Olympics after several practice runs on the local dry ski slope.

His fame went before him and a huge, cheering crowd met him at the airport, where his plane arrived late and his bag split open so that every piece of his gear went round and round the luggage carousel with Eddie in hot pursuit.

Next morning he found that his ski bindings had been crushed and so he missed his first two practice jumps while they were repaired. He got in one jump and survived, only to find that he was locked out of his cabin with all his clothes inside.

The Worst Batsman

Although Patrick Moore, the astronomer, has had some success as a bowler, thanks to his 'medium-paced leg breaks with a long, leaping, kangaroo-type action', we are prepared to overlook this in view of his outstanding contribution to the art of batting.

In a playing career which extends over half a century with the Lord's Taverners and his village team in Sussex, he has achieved a superb batting average of 0.8 runs an innings and has broken into double figures only once since 1949.

In his best season (1948) he scored only one run and that was from a dropped catch. That year he shattered the existing record for the most consecutive ducks (a measly eight) when he powered to a magnificent eighteen on the trot.

There are two possible explanations for his prowess. Mr Moore himself puts it down to having only two strokes, 'a cow shot to leg' and 'a desperate forward swat', which he uses in strict rotation. Furthermore, he does not wear spectacles when batting. 'Someone said it wouldn't make any difference if I wore binoculars.'

The Lowest Score in a Test Match

New Zealand achieved this unique honour in March 1955, when they scored a spectacular twenty-six against England at Auckland.

It is worth listing the score of the eleven great batsmen who shared the glory.

J. G. Leggatt	1
M. B. Poore	0
B. Sutcliffe	11
J. R. Reid	1
G. O. Rathbone	7
S. N. McGregor	1
H. B. Cave	5
A. R. MacGibbon	0
I. A. Colquhoun	0
A. M. Moir	0 (not out)
J. A. Hayes	0
Extras	0
	26

Sadly, the dismal England side did not enter into the spirit of things, and won by an innings and twenty runs.

Our Own Chess Master

To his utter amazement Mr Geoffrey Hosking, an Englishman studying at Moscow University, was invited to take part in the 1965 Baku International Chess Tournament.

It transpired that they were short of foreign players and a Russian friend had put his name forward on the strength of Hosking's vodka-fuelled victory in a casual friendly game that neither of them could remember with any clarity.

Hosking not only lost all twelve games in Baku, but also played them in such a way that the Tournament Bulletin refused to publish the customary match details on the grounds that they were not up to scratch.

The Fastest Defeat in Chess

Gibaud has been overthrown. Ever since 1924 this French chess master has been revered for achieving defeat in only four moves. A Monsieur Labard played the walk-on part in this great scene.

But in the 1959 US Open Championship somebody

called Masefield was a useful foil, moving around the white pieces in a match that enabled the immortal Trinka to be checkmated in three moves:

P–K4	P–KKt4
Kt–QB3	P–KB4
Q–R5	Mate

The Least Successful Golf Club

The City Golf Club in London is unique among such organizations in not possessing a golf course, ball, tee, caddy or bag. Its whole premises, just off Fleet Street, do not contain a single photograph of anything that approaches a golfing topic.

'We had a driving range once,' the commissionaire said, 'but we dropped that years ago.' The membership now devotes itself exclusively to eating and drinking.

The Least Successful Pigeon Race: 1

One great appeal of this sport is that during the race itself all you have to do is go home and wait.

Even under these ideal conditions, races can still go wrong. One of the most unsuccessful ever was held in 1978, when 6,745 racing pigeons were released at Preston in Lancashire. Of these 5,545 were never seen again.

'In all my forty years with racing pigeons,' said Mr James Paterson, secretary of the Ayrshire Federation of Homing Pigeons, 'I have never known anything like it. They have vanished. Someone suggested they might have flown over a grouse moor and been shot. I can't believe they could have got all 5,545.'

The most likely-sounding explanation was advanced by Mr Tony Soper, the naturalist. He said the birds may have gone to the Devonshire seaside, which sounds a very sensible thing to do.

The Least Successful Pigeon Race: 2

Nothing brings greater excitement to a pigeon race than the complete disappearance of all or most of the competitors.

The 1978 record was comprehensively shattered in 1983, when the Northern Ireland Pigeon Racing Society lost 16,430 in one go. Although a handful of duller birds flew straight home in record time, swarms of more adventurous little creatures were later found basking in country gardens all over West Wales. Housewives were asked to leave out rice, lentils and dried peas to build their strength up, but eventually special transport was laid on for the journey home.

The Least Successful Fishing Trip

It was the perfect day for fishing. Leaving his farm on the north Kent coast one bright Thursday in August 1981, Mr John Jenkins took his family to the nearby resort of Seasalter.

Three-quarters of a mile out on to the mudflats his four-wheel-drive Dodge got stuck. Mr Jenkins made the long trek back to a telephone and called out one of his tractors. As soon as it arrived, this got stuck as well. The family climbed out and watched as the tide covered both vehicles.

On the Friday morning the first tractor was pulled out by a second. Together they set off to rescue the Dodge, but *en route* both got stuck and were engulfed by the incoming tide.

Mr Jenkins now had three vehicles under water and so set out with his third tractor to remedy the situation. In rescuing the Dodge this tractor also became stuck and that night it too disappeared beneath the waves.

By Saturday morning word had spread of this great sea adventure and whole families travelled out across the mud to watch a mechanical digger arrive and release one tractor before itself becoming wedged in the mud. By Saturday night that was under water as well. On Sunday morning the rescued tractor went back to assist, whereupon it became immediately stuck in the mud and the tide covered the entire contents of Mr Jenkins's garage.

The Worst Homing Pigeon

This historic bird was released in Pembrokeshire in June 1953 and was expected to reach its base that evening.

It was returned by post, dead, in a cardboard box, eleven years later from Brazil. 'We had given it up for lost,' its owner said.

The Least Successful Birdwatchers

In November 1986 200 birdwatchers from all over Britain gathered in the Scilly Isles to see the arrival of an extremely rare grey-cheeked thrush. During the long wait they discussed the bird's North African habitat, its exquisite colouring and the precise detail of its unusually melodious call.

Peering through binoculars, they saw the priceless bird fly in amidst exclamations regarding its beauty. As soon as it landed on the campsite at St Mary's Garrison Mrs S. Burrows' cat, Muffin, dashed out, snatched the thrush in its mouth, disappeared into a bush and brought the birdwatching session to a close.

The Worst Bet

Just before the First World War Mr Horatio Bottomley, the British politican and horse owner, carefully devised what he considered to be a sure way of winning a fortune.

His plan was beautifully simple: prior to a race at Blankenberghe in Belgium, he bought all six horses entered. He then hired six English jockeys, who were given strict instructions as to the order in which they should cross the finishing line. Leaving nothing to chance, Bottomley backed all the horses, as a final precaution.

All was going smoothly until half-way through the race, when a thick sea mist blew inshore and engulfed the whole course. Jockeys could not see each other and judges could not see the horses, and those that finished at all did so in a hopeless jumble.

Mr Bottomley lost a fortune.

The Worst Angler

Thomas Birch, the eighteenth-century scholar, was a keen fisherman. However, he rarely caught anything and so decided to disguise himself in order to lull the fish into a false sense of security.

He constructed an outfit which made him look like a tree. His arms fitted into the branches and his eyes peered through knots in the bark.

Thus attired, he set off down the riverbank and took up his position. He still did not catch anything, attracting only suspicious dogs and friends, who used to picnic at his feet.

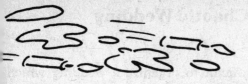

And They Lived
Happily Ever After

The Most Chaotic Wedding Ceremony

It would be difficult to organize a wedding which ran less smoothly than the one held in July 1973 at Kingston in Surrey.

For a start the vicar went sick and they had to rustle up a pastoral replacement to seal the knot at short notice. Matters worsened considerably when the groom put the ring on his bride's finger and she had a blackout. She remained unconscious for twenty minutes.

While she was carried off and revived, the choir sang 'Jesu, Joy of Man's Desiring' to disguise a welter of fanning, slapping and blowing.

Once the bride had regained consciousness the ceremony was completed. The happy couple made their way down the aisle. In a shower of nuts and confetti, they approached the going-away car, which was now seen to contain a cement-mixer. The groom took this opportunity to tell guests that the honeymoon hotel had burnt down and instead they were going to spend the time building a septic tank.

Strangely modest, the couple have asked to remain unnamed.

The Least Successful Wedding Cake

Your wedding is a day to remember and Signor Enrico Faldini of Naples is unlikely to forget his. At the reception during 1981 the wedding cake exploded when a waiter was lighting the candles, with the result that two guests, two waiters and a tourist taking a photograph of Signora Faldini were treated for shock.

Credit here goes to the chef, who later said: 'I think I must have used too much alcohol in the mix.'

The Most Unsuccessful Attempt to Propose Marriage

In the late 1900s a teacher in London was enamoured of a well-to-do young woman called Gwendolin, who lived in Sussex. One weekend he went to the family's ancestral home near Lewes to ask her to marry him. On his first night he woke at 3 a.m. wanting a glass of water. Feeling his way to the basin in the dark he knocked something over. Next morning he awoke to find that he had spilt ink over the priceless fourteenth-century tapestry which was the pride and joy of Gwendolin's mother. He left immediately without seeing his beloved.

After the fuss had died down he returned to make another attempt. In order to minimize the chances of disaster he decided to call in for just half an hour in the afternoon. He asked Gwendolin's mother if he might speak to her daughter. While she was out of the room he sat down on what he took to be a cushion. It was, however, the family Pekinese, which did not survive the experience. He left again without seeing her. They both married other people.

The Least Whirlwind Romance

In 1900 Octavio Guillen met the girl who would one day be his wife. Two years later he announced his engagement to Adriana Martinez and everyone said they made a lovely couple.

They still made a lovely couple in 1969, when they cast caution to the wind and got married in Mexico City. They were both eighty-two and had been engaged for sixty-seven years.

The Least Ideal Couple

In 1983 a television company held a nationwide competition to find 'Britain's ideal couple'. The winning pair duly appeared in all the papers, smiling happily and giving extensive interviews about the secret of their successful relationship.

Had it ended there this unseemly bliss would merely have depressed the entire nation. The couple, however, turned out to be far more interesting than anyone would have suspected. The day before the programme was broadcast the young woman announced that their engagement was off because her fiancé had (a) smacked her face at a Lindisfarne concert and (b) kept from her the fact that he was already married to a woman called Barbara, who had thought that *they* were the ideal couple. The programme was broadcast as planned.

The Most Misspelt Name

Edward A. Nedelcov of Regina, Canada, smashed all records with an amazing 1,023 misspellings of his family name since January 1960. He finds that Nevelcove, Neddlecough, Middlecou and Needochou are quite common versions. However, a letter from Club Med. improved upon these by writing to Edward Nedle and Co. His bank addressed him once as Needleco and later as Nedleson. Even a telegram from a close friend in Sydney accepting a wedding invitation was addressed to B. Heddlegove.

On a receipt for nine extra-large spare ribs from Western Pizzas he was down as Meerinwoz. On a later receipt for nine extra-large chickens he was Petlecode. A third receipt said Nidcole and a fourth, Nuddlecale. At this point he switched to Romano Pizzas, who went for Nettlecove.

As a primary school teacher, he has now taken to including his own name in spelling tests. Amidst 'cat', 'bread' and 'please' he inserts 'Mr Nedelcov', with universally wayward results. Kevin Seivewright got it down as Mr Nettlecoke, while in her class diary Lisa Mae Clarke wrote: 'Today I started at Mabel Brown School. I am in room number one and my teacher's name is Nevelcod.'

He once wrote to the Queen telling her about his grade-seven children. His proudest possession is a reply from Her Majesty addressed to E. A. Dedelcov.

The Least Popular Christian Names

For many years Mr J. W. Leaver wrote annually to *The Times* with the twenty Christian names which had proven most popular around the font during the previous year. He at no point listed the twenty least popular. The following names were all used between 1838 and 1900, but now have fallen into spectacular neglect:

Abishag	Ham
Amorous	Lettuce
Babberley	Minniehaha
Brained	Murder
Bugless	Salmon
Clapham	Strongitharm
Despair	Tram
Dozer	Uz
Energetic	Water
Feather	Wonderful

How to Visit Loved Ones

The art of visiting relatives was significantly enhanced by Dr John Fellows of Dorset in March 1984. Having bought a £600 return air ticket to New York, he flew to John F. Kennedy Airport. On arrival, however, he found that he could not remember his daughter's address.

Most of us could have managed this, but Dr Fellows went one further and found that he was also unable to remember her name. Thus equipped, he spent several hours at the airport trying to recall it before catching the next plane home. 'I was tired,' he explained.

The Worst Household Ornament

For thirty years Mrs Doreen Burley polished her favourite ornament every day. She allowed her five grandchildren to play with it and usually gave the brass orb pride of place on the mantelpiece at her home in Rawtenstall, Lancashire.

Only in March 1988 did she discover it was a live bomb. When she described her pride and joy to the manager of an antique shop, he advised her to call the police.

The army arrived next day and carried it off as though it was priceless china. 'I just couldn't believe I had been polishing a bomb all this time,' Mrs Burley said. 'I must have picked it up in a box of brasses in Bradford.'

Animal Snippets

The Least Successful Purchase of a Pet

In 1980 an Italian businessman in Brescia was sent out to buy a pet dog for his children. When he returned with a small fluffy bundle a family argument immediately broke out as to what breed it was. His wife insisted it was a fine-haired chihuahua and his children would not sleep for claiming it was a poodle, while the buyer himself would hear no word against his own belief that it was a pedigree Labrador, as the salesman had told him.

Only when they took the animal to the vet after three months, complaining that it never barked, did they learn that it was, in fact, a lion.

The Least Successful Lion

In 1970 a lion escaped from a circus in Italy. Typically, it found a small boy and started to chase him. Less typically, the small boy's mother turned on the lion and badly mauled it. The animal suffered severe head and skin wounds, and received treatment for shock.

The Least Successful Animal Rescue

The fireman's strike of 1978 made possible one of the great animal rescue attempts of all time. Valiantly, the British Army had taken over emergency firefighting and on 14 January they were called out by an elderly lady in south London to retrieve her cat, which had become trapped up a tree. They arrived with impressive haste and soon discharged their duty. So grateful was the lady that she invited them all in for tea. Driving off later, with fond farewells completed, they ran over the cat and killed it.

The Worst Rescue Dog

A key member of the mountain rescue team in the village of Valchiusella in the northern Italian Alps was Bruno, a St Bernard dog with a genius for getting lost.

Bursting with enthusiasm, he always raced on ahead. Once, in 1980, it took a second search party longer to recover Bruno than the climbers he was trying to find. This was the eighth time in two years that Bruno had been rescued, and the ideal moment to bring his great career to an end.

Snippets

'Animals, which move, have limbs and muscles. The earth does not have limbs and muscles; therefore it does not move' – Scipio Chiaramonti.